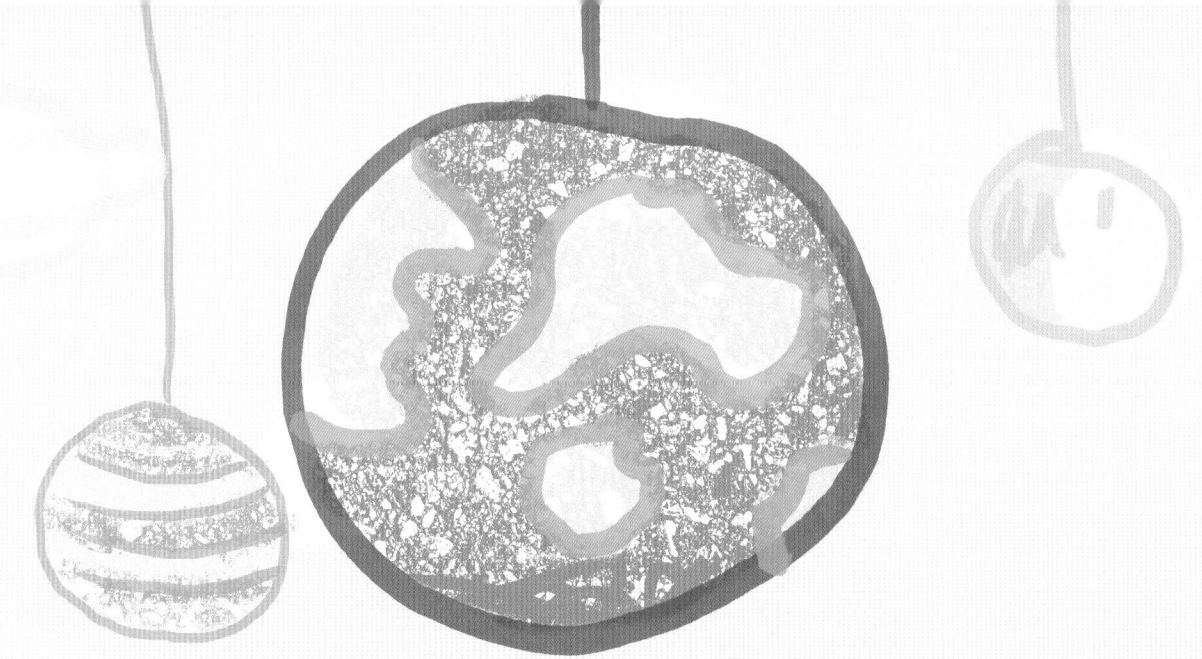

For Mom and Dad — M.N.
For Nan and Tom — L.C.

# You and Me Both

WRITTEN BY
**Mahtab Narsimhan**

ILLUSTRATED BY
**Lisa Cinar**

Owlkids Books

Jamal
loves
building
tall block
towers...

And
knocking
them
down.

So do I!!

I love
strawberry
jam
on
toast.

He gobbles
it up
too!

Carrots are yuck!

Jamal showed me how to feed them to **the rabbit.**

Our teacher is so happy with our clean plates.

When it rains,
we race to
find the largest
puddles.

Our matching boots go **splish, splash, splat!**

At nap time, Jamal wants the **crocodile** pillow.

I want  it too.

Its jaws are big enough for both of us.

# Fuzzy Tales
## is our
## favorite show.

We both want dogs, but our moms said no.

# When Jamal gets a haircut,

# Our teacher will never tell us apart now.

# When it's time to go home, **I'm sad.**

Jamal is
also sad.

Saying goodbye
is hard.

Twins
should always
stick
together.

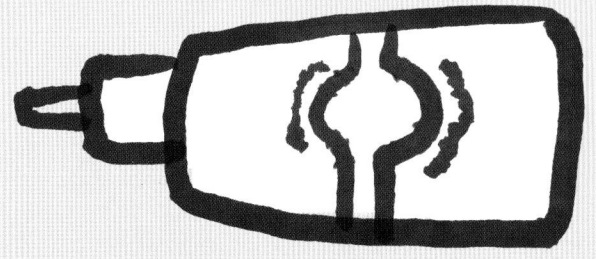

Owlkids Books acknowledges the financial support of the Canada Council for the Arts, the Ontario Arts Council, the Government of Canada through the Canada Book Fund (CBF) and the Government of Ontario through the Ontario Creates Book Initiative for our publishing activities.

Published in Canada by Owlkids Books Inc., 1 Eglinton Avenue East, Toronto, ON M4P 3A1
Published in the US by Owlkids Books Inc., 1700 Fourth Street, Berkeley, CA 94710

Library of Congress Control Number: 2019947248

Library and Archives Canada Cataloguing in Publication

Title: You and me both / written by Mahtab Narsimhan ; illustrated by Lisa Cinar.
Names: Narsimhan, Mahtab, author. | Cinar, Lisa, 1980- illustrator.
Identifiers: Canadiana 20190162813 | ISBN 9781771473668 (hardcover)
Classification: LCC PS8627.A77 Y68 2020 | DDC jC813/.6-dc23

Edited by Karen Li | Designed by Lisa Cinar and Alisa Baldwin

Manufactured in Johor Bahru, Johor, Malaysia, in October 2019, by Tien Wah Press
Job #57447

A     B     C     D     E     F

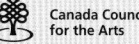

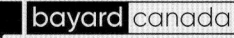

ONTARIO ARTS COUNCIL
CONSEIL DES ARTS DE L'ONTARIO
an Ontario government agency
un organisme du gouvernement de l'Ontario

Canada Council
for the Arts
Conseil des Arts
du Canada

Canadä

Owl kids
Publisher of Chirp, Chickadee and OWL
www.owlkidsbooks.com     |     Owlkids Books is a division of     bayard canada

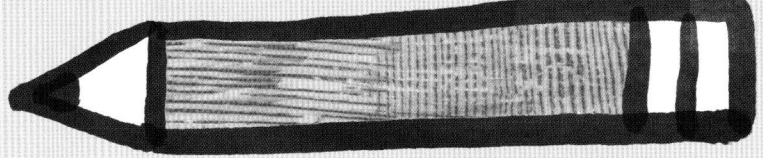

23